She soon spies Guy the fly outside.

KU-637-143

"I didn't do it," Guy replies.
"Please listen. I'll explain."

"It all began with Slug..." says Guy.
"I saw him by the lake.

The Fly who told a Lie

Russell Punter
Illustrated by Siân Roberts

WALTHAM FOREST LIBRARIES

904 000 00756726

Bee is making honey buns when...

CRASH!

THUD!

What was that?

She buzzes off to see what's wrong.

A ball lies on her mat.

Then Dragonfly
swooped down on him...

and stole his
creamy cake.

Dragonfly whizzed off so fast... she zoomed right into Toad.

The cake went flying from her grasp...

and landed on the road.

Beetle skidded through the cream.

It's slippery as soap!

She stumbled, tumbled, lost her grip...

and bounced right down a slope.

She crashed,
SLAP! BANG!
against a tree.

Down came a
hornets' nest.

"Who smashed our lovely home?" wailed one.

"THAT BEETLE!" yelled the rest.

"I couldn't help it!"
Beetle screamed.

"Come back!" the hornets cried.

She jumped into a tractor, but...

These levers don't make sense!

Poor Beetle couldn't steer at all and...

CRASHED

straight through a fence.

The tractor chugged across a field.
A game was underway.

"Are you crazy?" cried the ants.
"Clear off and let us play!"

Beetle jumped out from the cab.
The tractor kept on going.

We had no way of knowing.

It crashed into a
storage shed...

and out the balls all came.

One flew
SKY HIGH...

BOUNCED on
the ground...

and SMASHED
your window pane.

So that's what happened," Guy concludes, "and every word is true."

Bee points to writing on the ball. "Does this belong to you?"

Guy starts mumbling. "Well..." he says.
"Now, no more lies," says Bee.

"Then do some chores instead," says Bee.

So Guy works hard all day.

He mops up spills and sweeps the floor.

Nice work, Guy. That's the way.

He cleans
Bee's car until
it gleams.

"That's looking good," cries Bee.

Guy's last job is cutting grass.

Come in and have some tea.

Designed by Laura Bridges and Laura Nelson Norris
Edited by Lesley Sims

This edition published in 2023 by Usborne Publishing Limited, 83-85 Saffron Hill, London EC1N 8RT, United Kingdom. usborne.com
Copyright © 2023, 2022 Usborne Publishing Limited. The name Usborne and the Balloon logo are registered trade marks of
Usborne Publishing Limited. All rights reserved. No part of this publication may be reproduced, stored in a retrieval system or
transmitted in any form or by any means without prior permission of the publisher. UKE.